Praise for CRITICAL CARE

"EXCELLENT . . . NOT FOR THE SQUEAMISH . . .
DOOLING SHOWS IN RARE DETAIL
HOW THE DEHUMANIZING OPERATION
OF AN INSTITUTION CHARGED WITH
PRESERVING HUMAN LIFE
CAN THWART ITS MISSION,
AND MAIM PHYSICIANS AND PATIENTS ALIKE."
San Diego Union–Tribune

"A BRUTALLY HONEST LOOK INTO
THE WORLD OF THE INTENSIVE CARE UNIT"
The Herald

"SIMPLY IMPOSSIBLE TO PUT DOWN . . .
CONSISTENTLY ABSORBING,
AS STUNNING AS ANY
STEPHEN KING HORROR STORY"
Bob Marion, M.D., *author of* The Intern Blues

"RIVETING . . . GUT-WRENCHINGLY ACCURATE,
AUTHENTICALLY FRIGHTENING
AND CERTAINLY TIMELY"
Publishers Weekly

"THE KIND OF SCATHINGLY TRAGICOMIC LOOK
AT AN INTENSIVE CARE UNIT
THAT THE ORIGINAL *M*A*S*H* TOOK AT
MILITARY MEDICINE."
St. Louis Post–Dispatch

"DOOLING TAKES THE CURRENT
HOSPITAL STEREOTYPES AND SETS THEM
ON THEIR EARS."
The Riverfront Times